The Sweetie Jar

by

Venell Mitchell

Illustrations by

Shannen Marie Paradero

Print information available on the last page

Rev. date: 04/11/2016

To order additional copies of this book, contact:
Xlibris
0800-056-3182
www.xlibrispublishing.co.uk
Orders@ Xlibrispublishing.co.uk

The book is dedicated to
my granddaughter,

Tia

One day, Tia and her Mum were walking along Chimber Street, when Tia spotted a sweet shop as they rounded a bend in the road.

"Hi, Mum! there's a sweet shop. Please can we go in?" "Alright then," said Mum. "Just for a few minutes, as you have been a very helpful girl today." "Thank you, Mummy," said Tia with glee, as they enter the shop.

On a red counter near the door stood a sweetie jar full of delicious looking sweets of different shapes and colours.

Tia's eyes opened wide as she stared at the jar of sweets.

There were yellow ones, red ones, green ones, brown ones and multicoloured ones, all packed in the jar.

Suddenly, Tia heard a voice coming from inside the sweetie jar. One of the sweeties had started to speak. It was round as a ball and had the colour of an orange.

"Hello, Tia!" said the sweetie ball. "My name is CHUPA CHUPS and I am a lollipop. I am glad to see you today. Would you like to buy me and take me home? I would taste so good, just like an orange, and you can have me after dinner."

Before Tia could reply,

there came another voice from the sweetie jar.

"Hi, Tia!" it said, "Look at me. I am TRAFFIC LIGHT and

I am also a lollipop, but someone attached me to a stick.
I am in the colours of the traffic lights that you see on the
street that help people to cross the road safely. My colours
are red, green and yellow. Aren't I cute? Would you like
to try me? Just take me by my stick and give me a lick.
You will love my taste."

CHUPA CHUPS
FRIED EGG
PINEAPPLE FIZ
CHOCOLATE
BON-BON

TRAFFIC LIGHT
COLA BOTTLE
PEAR DROP
JELLY BABY
BANANA FLUMP

TRAFFIC LIGHT

Tia was amazed at what was taking place in the sweetie jar. She didn't know what to say. As she turned to her Mum, she heard a little squeaky voice coming from the bottom of the jar.

"Good day, Tia! My name is JELLY BABY. Don't I look nice in my bright red outfit? I am soft and chewy and I taste yummy. You will have no trouble eating me for I would just melt in your mouth."

Tia bent over the sweetie jar to have a closer look at the sweets.

There was BANANA FLUMP, yellow and shaped like a banana.

There was PINEAPPLE FIZ, also yellow but oval shaped .

There was COLA BOTTLE which was brown at the bottom and clear at the top.

There were PEAR DROPS in pretty colours and shaped like pears that we buy from the fruit shop.

CHOCOLATE BON BON was dark brown and as round as a marble.

And there was FRIED EGG which Tia thought was a real egg for it looked just like one.

Tia shouted to her Mum to come and have a look at FRIED EGG. "Why is it in the sweetie jar?" asked Tia. Mum explained that although FRIED EGG looked like a real egg, it was also a sweetie, but in the shape and colours of a fried egg.

Tia could not make up her mind which one of the sweeties she should buy, for they all looked so scrumptious in the sweetie jar.

When the sweeties saw that Tia could not decide which of them to buy and take home with her, they all started calling out to her. "Buy me, Tia," said BANANA FLUMP. "Please try me," blurted out COLA BOTTLE.

"Oh Tia! You would like my fizzy taste," shouted PINEAPPLE FIZ. "I would just fizzle away in your mouth."

" Yum Yum," yelled PEAR DROP, "I am super tasty."

"I am the best," squealed CHOCOLATE BON BON. "I taste milky and will last forever."

"Oh dear," said the sweetie jar to Tia. "You are in a quandary. Shall I help you?" "Yes please," said Tia. "What you should do," suggested the sweetie jar," is to buy one of each of my sweeties, then everyone will be happy."

"That's a good idea," said Tia, "but I'll have to ask my Mum first."

CHUPA CHUPS
FRIED EGG
PINEAPPLE FIZ
CHOCOLATE
BON-BON

TRAFFIC LIGHT
COLA BOTTLE
PEAR DROP
JELLY BABY
BANANA FLUMP

Tia asked Mum if she could have one of each of the sweeties in the sweetie jar.

Mum said yes, but told her she must have only one sweetie a day after dinner.

Tia collected the sweeties and Mum gave her the money to pay the shop man. He packed them in a pretty little box and handed it to Tia.

As Tia and her Mum were leaving the shop, the sweetie jar said, "Goodbye, Tia. Hope to see you again." And Tia replied, "Goodbye, Sweetie Jar. Thank you, and have a good day."

THE END

ABOUT THE AUTHOR

Venell Mitchell is a Mother and Grandmother who was born and grew up in the West Indies. She migrated to the UK in the seventies, where she currently resides. For quite some time she has harboured a desire to write a children's book and this one is her first attempt.

The idea for this book was conceived a few years ago after having purchased some sweets from an online confectionery store, at a time she was babysitting her granddaughter.